JUST SO STORIES

How the Rhinoceros got his Skin

by
Rudyard Kipling

Illustrated by Peter Bowman

How the Rhinoceros got his Skin from *Just So Stories*
first published in 1902
Copyright text the National Trust

This edition first published in Great Britain in 1984 by

Octopus Books Limited
59 Grosvenor Street
London W1

by arrangement with Macmillan Children's Books,
a division of Macmillan Publishers Limited

ISBN 0 7064 2208 2

Illustrations and arrangement © 1984 Octopus Books Limited

Produced by

Mandarin Publishers Limited
22a Westlands Road
Quarry Bay, Hong Kong

Printed and bound in Spain by
Graficas Estella

nce upon a time, on an uninhabited island on the shores of the Red Sea, there lived a Parsee from whose hat the rays of the sun were reflected in more-than-oriental splendour.

nd the Parsee lived by the Red Sea with nothing but his hat and his knife and a cooking-stove of the kind that you must particularly never touch. And one day he took flour and water and currants and plums and sugar and things, and made himself one cake which was two feet across and three feet thick. It was indeed a Superior Comestible (*that's* Magic), and he put it on the stove because *he* was allowed to cook on that stove, and he baked it and he baked it till it was all done brown and smelt most sentimental.

ut just as he was going to eat it there came down to the beach from the Altogether Uninhabited Interior one Rhinoceros with a horn on his nose, two piggy eyes, and few manners. In those days the Rhinoceros's skin fitted him quite tight. There were no wrinkles in it anywhere.

 e looked exactly like a Noah's Ark Rhinoceros, but of course much bigger. All the same, he had no manners then, and he has no manners now, and he never will have any manners. He said,

'How!' and the Parsee left that cake and climbed to the top of a palm-tree with nothing on but his hat, from which the rays of the sun were always reflected in more-than-oriental splendour.

nd the Rhinoceros upset the oil-stove with his nose, and the cake rolled on the sand, and he spiked that cake on the horn of his nose, and he ate it, and he went away, waving his tail, to the desolate and Exclusively Uninhabited Interior which abuts on the islands of Mazanderan, Socotra, and the Promontories of the Larger Equinox.

hen the Parsee came down from his palm-tree and put the stove on its legs and recited the following Sloka, which, as you have not heard, I will now proceed to relate: —

'Them that takes cakes
Which the Parsee man bakes
Makes dreadful mistakes.'

And there was a great deal
more in that than you would
think.

Because, five weeks later,
there was a heat-wave in the
Red Sea, and everybody took
off all the clothes they had.

 he Parsee took off his hat; the Rhinoceros took off his skin and carried it over his shoulder as he came down to the beach to bathe. In those days it buttoned underneath with three buttons and looked like a waterproof.

 e said nothing whatever
about the Parsee's cake,
because he had eaten it
all; and he never had any
manners, then, since, or hence-
forward. He waddled straight
into the water and blew bubbles

through his nose, leaving his skin on the beach.

Presently the Parsee came by and found the skin, and he smiled one smile that ran all round his face two times. Then he danced three times round the skin and rubbed his hands.

hen he went to his camp and filled his hat with cake-crumbs, for the Parsee never ate anything but cake, and never swept out his camp.

e took that skin, and he shook that skin, and he scrubbed that skin, and he rubbed that skin just as full of old, dry, stale, tickly cake-crumbs and some burned currants as ever it could *possibly* hold.

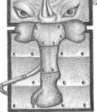

hen he climbed to the top of his palm-tree and waited for the Rhinoceros to come out of the water and put it on.

And the Rhinoceros did. He buttoned it up with the three buttons, and it tickled like cake-crumbs in bed. Then he wanted to scratch, but that made it worse; and then he lay down on the sands and rolled and rolled and rolled, and every time he rolled the cake-crumbs tickled him worse and worse and worse.

hen he ran to the palm-tree and rubbed and rubbed and rubbed himself against it. He rubbed so much and so hard that he rubbed his skin into a great fold over his shoulders, and another fold underneath, where the buttons used to be (but he rubbed the buttons off), and he rubbed some more folds over his legs.

nd it spoiled his temper, but it didn't make the least difference to the cake-crumbs. They were inside his skin and they tickled. So he went home, very angry

32

indeed and horribly scratchy; and from that day to this every rhinoceros has great folds in his skin and a very bad temper, all on account of the cake-crumbs inside.

ut the Parsee came down from his palm-tree, wearing his hat, from which the rays of the sun were reflected in more-than-oriental splendour, packed up his cooking-stove, and went away in the direction of Oro-tavo, Amygdala, and the Upland Meadows of Antana-narivo, and the Marshes of Sonaput.

THE END